HIS BODY CAN

Published by Greenleaf Book Group Press
Austin, Texas
www.gbgpress.com

Distributed by Greenleaf Book Group

For ordering information or special discounts for bulk purchases, please contact Greenleaf Book Group at PO Box 91869, Austin, TX 78709, 512.891.6100.

Design and composition by Greenleaf Book Group and Krista Huber
Cover design by Greenleaf Book Group and Krista Huber
Illustrations by Li Liu

Publisher's Cataloging-in-Publication data is available.

Print ISBN: 978-1-62634-893-6

eBook ISBN: 978-1-62634-894-3

Part of the Tree Neutral® program, which offsets the number of trees consumed in the production and printing of this book by taking proactive steps, such as planting trees in direct proportion to the number of trees used: www.treeneutral.com

Manufactured through Guangzhou Hangtong Packing Product Ltd
Manufactured in China on January 3, 2022

22 23 24 25 26 27   10 9 8 7 6 5 4 3 2 1
First Edition

HIS BODY CAN

From #1 BESTSELLING AUTHORS

Katie Crenshaw & Ady Meschke

Illustrated by Li Liu

GREENLEAF
BOOK GROUP PRESS

For Colton
Dream big, sweet boy.
Always hold on to your carefree spirit and celebrate who you are.
I will always love you.
—A.M.

For Grayson and Lincoln
Always remember that you get to be the main character in your story.
Trust your truthand allow yourself to be exactly who you want to be.
—K.C.

His body can scream,
cheer, laugh, or cry.

Feelings are good to express all the time.

His body can choose pants, shorts or a suit

But kilts and pink dresses can also be cute!

His body can rock a spikey new do...

Braids, curls and buns
are all okay too.

His body can
do crunches, lift weights and do pushups.

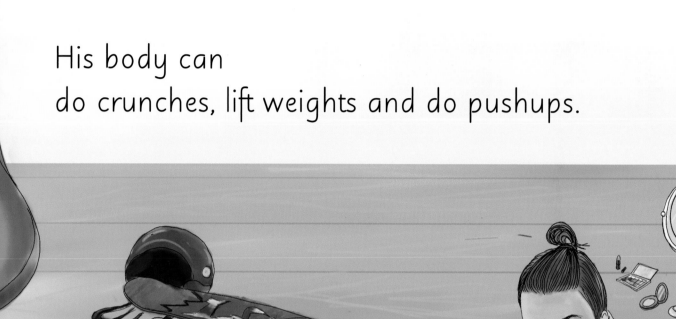

He might also like crafts, dancing, reading and makeup.

His body can play the best ball in the land

Or he might want to play
the best flute in the band.

His body can eat all the burgers he wishes.

Pastries and fruits are also delicious.

His body can yell really loud like a giant.

Or squeak like a mouse, or even be silent.

His body can be tall,
short, skinny or round.

All bodies are awesome wherever they're found.

His body can stand up to bullies at school.

It's not okay to hurt feelings. Kindness is cool.

His body can ace all the quizzes and tests.

But that's not required to be one of the best.

His body can wrestle, get rough and be wild.

Or maybe he's happiest mellow and mild.

His body can cook, clean,

mend and garden.

Being a boy doesn't
give helping a pardon.

His body is his. He'll be who he decides.

Worth is

within him.

There's no need to hide.

His body can help him create his own joy.

There's no one more you
than you, sweet boy.

Dear Reader,

In today's world, gender-based expectations begin very early in life. From media influence to ingrained generational beliefs, boys commonly feel pressure to behave, dress, and play in certain ways.

Through the rhymes and illustrations in this book, we hope to assure both children and parents that there are no rules when it comes to what we love or how we are most comfortable expressing who we are. The best versions of all of us are the unique beings we are designed to be.

Our wish for this book is to empower all boys—young and old—that you are free to color outside the lines, think outside the box of "masculinity" and help rewrite the cultural narriative on what it means to "be a boy."

Love, K & A

ABOUT THE AUTHORS

Ady Meschke and Katie Crenshaw are Atlanta-based bloggers and mothers working to redefine gender norms through honest conversations with their followers.

Ady is an award-winning travel blogger for Verbal Gold Blog, and a body-inclusive activewear mogul who has been featured in national publications such as Shape and The Today Show. To learn more about Ady and her mission, follow her on Instagram @verbalgoldblog or visit her website at www.verbalgoldblog.com

Katie is a nationally recognized body-positivity and mental health spokesperson who has been featured on Good Morning America, CNN and Inside Edition, and is the 2020 spokesperson for The Blue Dot Project. To learn more about Katie and her mission, follow her on Instagram @katiemcrenshaw or visit her website at www.katiecrenshaw.com